Billie B. Brown

www.BillieBBrownBooks.com

Billie B. Brown Books

The Bad Butterfly
The Soccer Star
The Midnight Feast
The Second-best Friend
The Extra-special Helper
The Beautiful Haircut
The Big Sister
The Spotty Vacation
The Birthday Mix-up
The Secret Message
The Little Lie
The Best Project
The Deep End
The Copycat Kid
The Night Fright

First American Edition 2015
Kane Miller, A Division of EDC Publishing

Text copyright © 2012 Sally Rippin
Illustrations copyright © 2012 Aki Fukuoka
First published in Australia in 2012 by Hardie Grant Egmont

For information contact:
Kane Miller, A Division of EDC Publishing
P.O. Box 470663
Tulsa, OK 74147-0663
www.kanemiller.com
www.edcpub.com
www.usbornebooksandmore.com

Library of Congress Control Number: 2014950304

Printed and bound in the United States of America
5 6 7 8 9 10

ISBN: 978-1-61067-391-4

The
Night
Fright

By Sally Rippin

Illustrated by Aki Fukuoka

A DIVISION OF EDC PUBLISHING

Chapter One

Billie B. Brown has one pair of 3-D glasses, one fizzy drink and a huge bucket of popcorn. Do you know what the "B" in Billie B. Brown stands for?

Buzzing.

Billie B. Brown is
buzzing with excitement.
She is going to the
movies with Rebecca
and her sisters.
Rebecca is in Billie's
class at school. She has
two big sisters called
Karri and Jen.

One pair of 3-D glasses

One fizzy drink

A huge bucket
of popcorn

Billie wishes she
had two big sisters.
Billie only has a fat baby
brother called Noah.
He is nice for cuddles
but not much else.

Rebecca's mom lines
up for the tickets.
"Which movie do you
want to see?" she asks.

"How about that one with the dancing mice?"

"Nah," says Jen. "That's for babies. Let's go and see the one about the haunted house."

"Hmmm," says Rebecca's mom. "It looks a bit scary."

"No, it's not," says Karri. "It's only PG. It's for kids."

"Well, I think we should let Billie and Rebecca decide," says Rebecca's mom.

"Are you OK with scary movies?" Jen asks Billie.

"Of course!" Billie says, though secretly she is a teensy bit **nervous**. Billie doesn't like scary movies much. They give her nightmares. But Billie doesn't want Rebecca's sisters to know this.

She wants them to think she is **brave**.

"Rebecca?" asks Rebecca's mom. "Are you OK with the scary movie?"

At first, Billie thinks Rebecca looks a bit nervous too. But then she says, "Sure! We're not babies, Mom."

"I *used* to get scared," Billie says in a big voice. "But that was when I was little, not now."

Karri and Jen laugh.

Billie grins. She likes
making Rebecca's big
sisters laugh.

"All right, then,"
says Rebecca's mom.
She buys the tickets and
walks them to the door.
"I'll pick you up here
when the movie is over.

Jen and Karri, look after Rebecca and Billie, OK?"

Billie grins. She is so  **excited** to be going to the movies with Rebecca and her two big sisters!

Chapter Two

Billie follows Rebecca and her sisters into the theater. They find their seats.

"Can I sit next to you?" Karri asks Billie.

"Sure!" says Billie.
She feels her cheeks
get hot with pride.
Rebecca's big sister
wants to sit next to *her!*

Karri leans in close and
shares Billie's popcorn.
Billie imagines what it
would be like if Karri
was *her* big sister. It is a
nice feeling.

Soon it is time for the movie to start. Everyone puts on their 3-D glasses. "Look!" Rebecca **squeals**. "The pictures are coming right out of the screen!"

Jen leans forward. "Shh!" she says. "Not so loud!"

But Billie and Rebecca wriggle with **excitement**. They wriggle and giggle so much that Billie nearly drops her popcorn on the floor.

"Careful!" says Karri. She catches the bucket just in time.

In the movie, two children
go to stay with their aunt
for the holidays. They take
their dog Fido with them.

Fido is very funny.
He makes everyone in the
theater laugh. But soon
the children find out their
aunt's house is haunted.
They walk into a little
room, which is dark
and **scary**. They open
up a cupboard.

Suddenly ghosts fly
out of the cupboard.

It looks like they are
coming out of the screen!
Billie **squeals** and
covers her eyes. Her heart
is beating very fast. She
sneaks a peek at Rebecca.

Rebecca is covering her eyes too.

Finally, the ghosts go away. The children search the house with their dog. The dog rolls around and chases his tail. He is very funny. Everyone in the theater laughs. Billie and Rebecca laugh the **loudest** of all.

"Shh!" say Karri and Jen together. "You two are being too noisy."

But Billie and Rebecca have got the giggles.

If Rebecca looks at Billie
she bursts out laughing.
If Billie looks at Rebecca,
she laughs too.

"I'll tell Mom," Karri says.

Rebecca rolls her eyes
at Billie. "Big sisters,"
she whispers. "They are
so annoying! You are lucky
you don't have them."

But Billie thinks Karri
and Jen are wonderful.

When the movie is over,
Rebecca's mom meets
them at the door.

"How was the movie?" she asks. "Not too scary?"

"It was hardly scary at all," boasts Billie. She and Rebecca look at each other and burst into giggles again.

Rebecca's mom smiles. "Well, I'm glad you girls had fun. We'll have to take you home now, Billie. But you might like to come again another day?"

"Yay!" says Rebecca.

Billie grins. She is so full of fizzy buzzy **happiness** she can hardly keep still.

Chapter Three

That night, Billie's mom tucks her into bed.

"Did you have fun with Rebecca today?" she asks.

"The best!" says Billie.

"We went to see a movie with her two big sisters."

"Oh, did you?" says Billie's mom. "Which movie?"

"The one about the haunted house," says Billie.

"Isn't that one a bit scary?" says her mom. She seems surprised. "I thought you didn't like scary movies."

"*Mom!*" says Billie.
"I'm not a *baby*."

Billie's mom smiles. "Good night then, my big girl."

Billie snuggles into bed and falls asleep.

Soon she begins to
dream. In her dream
she is in an old house.
It is dark and **scary**.
Doors creak and cobwebs
stick in her hair.

Billie hears someone
crying in the next room.
It's Noah! Billie doesn't
know what to do.
She wants to run away.

But what if Noah is in trouble? Billie slowly opens the door.

Suddenly, out flies a ghost! Then another and another!

Billie **screams** loudly.
Then she sits up.

"Mom!" she calls. "Mom!"

Billie's mom comes
rushing in. She has Noah
in her arms. "What's the
matter?" she says.

Billie's heart is pounding.
"I had a bad dream!" she says.
"There were ghosts.
And Noah was crying.

I thought the ghosts had taken him."

"Oh, Billie," says her mom. She gives Billie a cuddle. "I think that movie gave you nightmares. Look, Noah is right here. And he is perfectly fine. Aren't you, Noah?"

Noah giggles and holds out his soft fat arms.

Billie scoops him up into
a cuddle. She is so happy
to see that he is all right.
She kisses him on both
his fat cheeks.

"I love you to bits,"
she whispers in his ear.
Noah might be annoying
sometimes, but she
wouldn't swap him for all
the sisters in the world.

Billie looks up at
her mom. "Do you think
I could sleep in your
bed tonight?" she says.

"Just this once," says Billie's mom. "But no more scary movies, OK?"

Chapter Four

The next day at school
Billie sees Rebecca in the
playground. She is sitting
with Ella and Tracey.
When Rebecca sees
Billie she waves her over.

"Hey, Billie!" Rebecca calls. "How fun was the movie yesterday?"

"It was awesome," says Billie, laughing **nervously**. "The ghosts looked like they were coming out of the screen!"

Billie doesn't tell them about her nightmare. They might think she is silly.

"Which movie did you see?" asks Tracey.

"The one about the haunted house," says Rebecca.

"Oh, there's no way I'm going to that one," says Ella. "I hate scary movies."

"Me too," says Tracey. "They give me nightmares."

Billie is **surprised**.

"Me too!" she blurts. "I mean, when I was little I used to get nightmares," she says quickly.

38

She still doesn't want
Rebecca to think she
was scared of the film.

"I had nightmares
last night," Rebecca says
quietly. "I had to sleep in
my mom and dad's bed!"

"Really?" Billie **gasps**.
She can't believe it. "But I
thought you saw scary
movies all the time?"

"I do!" says Rebecca. "But only because Karri and Jen want to watch them. I like funny movies best."

"Me too," says Ella. "My favorite movie is *Finding Nemo.*"

"I love it too!" says Tracey.

"My sisters hate watching cartoons," Rebecca sighs. "They say cartoons are for babies. I always have to watch what they want to watch."

"You can come and watch *Finding Nemo* at my place," says Billie shyly. 'I've got it on DVD."

41

"Cool!" says Rebecca. "That would be awesome."

"Can we come too?" ask Tracey and Ella. "We could have a Nemo party!"

"Sure," says Billie. "I'll ask my mom. But we'll have to wait until Noah is in bed. The shark gives him nightmares!"

43

Collect them all!